THIS **Elephant & Piggie** BOOK
BELONGS TO:

To Jon Scieszka
(who also can't dance)

First published in Great Britain 2023 by Walker Books Ltd
87 Vauxhall Walk, London SE11 5HJ

First published in the USA by Disney-Hyperion
British publication rights arranged with Wernick & Pratt Agency, LLC

2 4 6 8 10 9 7 5 3 1

This book has been typeset in Century 725 and Grilled Cheese

Printed in China

British Library Cataloguing in Publication Data:
a catalogue record for this book is available from the British Library

ISBN 978-1-5295-1235-9 (paperback)
ISBN 978-1-5295-1590-9 (hardback)

www.walker.co.uk

An Elephant & Piggie Book

Elephants Cannot Dance!

Mo Willems

WALKER BOOKS
AND SUBSIDIARIES
LONDON • BOSTON • SYDNEY • AUCKLAND

Gerald!

Let's dance!

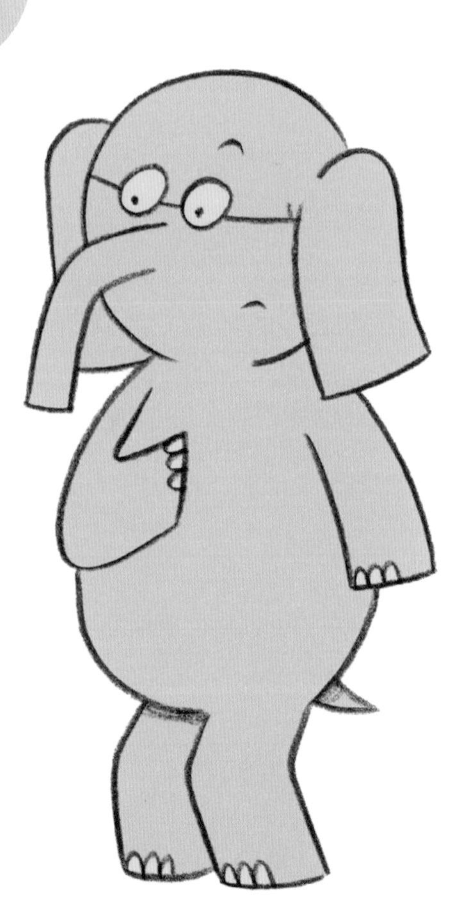

I can teach you!

I am teaching
all my friends.

I would love to
learn how to dance.

But elephants cannot dance.

You are kidding me.
No.

Look it up.

Page 11.

Gerald, it does not say
that you cannot *try*!

You are right, Piggie!

I *can* try to dance!

I *will* try to dance!

zip!

LET'S DANCE!

Oof!

OK. Let's go.

Jump with me when
I count to three.

One!

Two!

Three!

JUMP!

JUMP!

You were a little late on the jump.
I was a little late on the jump.

We will
try again.

We will
try again.

Move your arms
this way.

We will
try again.

We will
try again.

Lift your leg this way.

We will
try again.

We will
try again.

Up!
Up?

Down!
Down?

Spin!
Spin?

Stop!
Stop?

Forwards!

Forwards?

Backwards?
Backwards!

Wiggle-waggle!
Wiggle-waggle?

Robot walk!

Robot walk?!

ENOUGH!

I HAVE TRIED!
AND TRIED!
GROAN!
GRR!
GRUNT!

AND TRIED!

AND TRIED!

AND TRIED!

But I am
an elephant.

And elephants
just cannot dance.

PLOP!

Oh, Gerald...

Hello-o-o-o-o-o-o!

We are ready
to learn some
moves!

I am sorry. I cannot teach you now.

My friend is sad.

Silly! We do not want *you* to teach us!

We want to learn "The Elephant"!

Teach me, please!

Me too!

Me three!

More feeling!

Keep trying!

You are getting it!

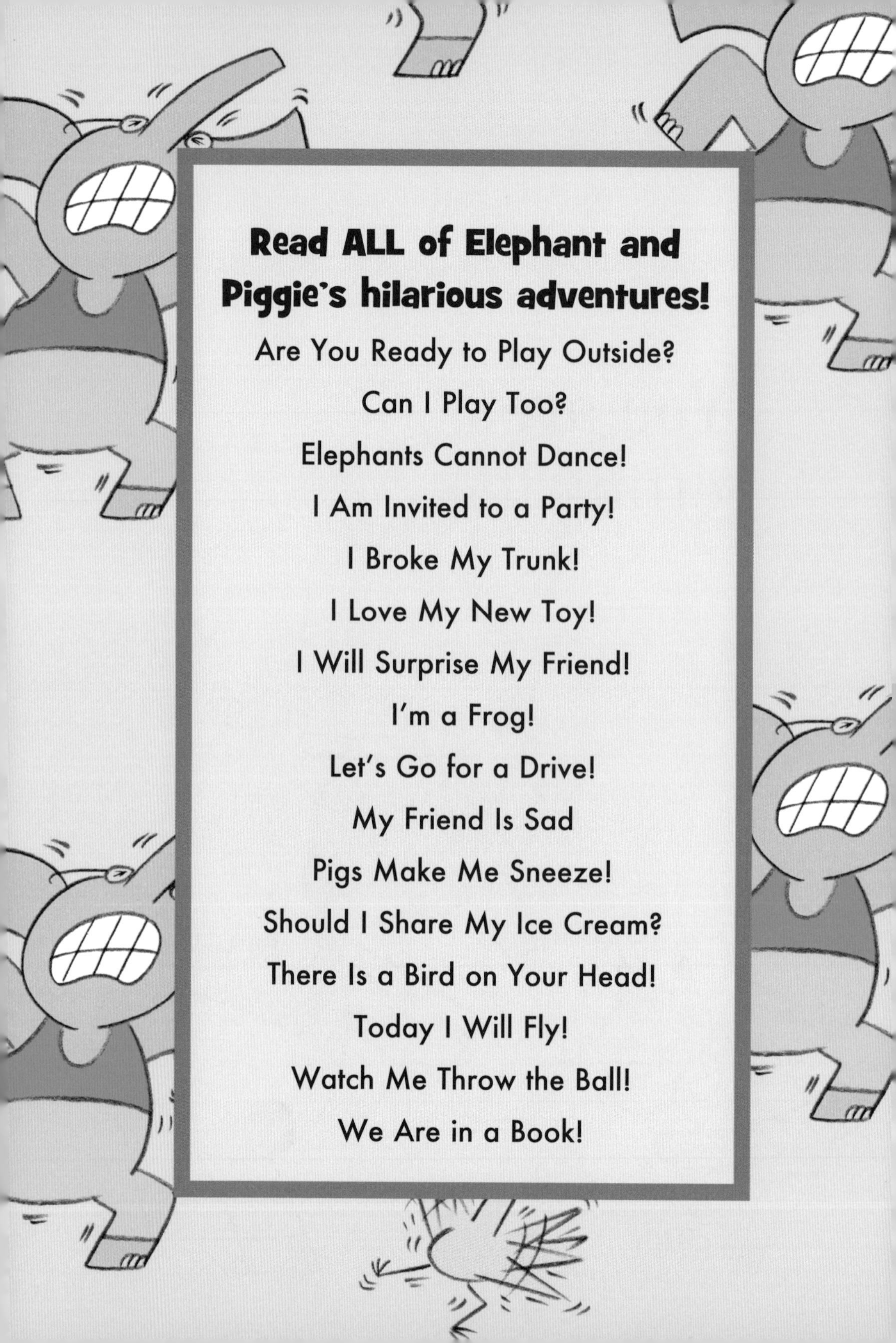

Read ALL of Elephant and Piggie's hilarious adventures!

Are You Ready to Play Outside?

Can I Play Too?

Elephants Cannot Dance!

I Am Invited to a Party!

I Broke My Trunk!

I Love My New Toy!

I Will Surprise My Friend!

I'm a Frog!

Let's Go for a Drive!

My Friend Is Sad

Pigs Make Me Sneeze!

Should I Share My Ice Cream?

There Is a Bird on Your Head!

Today I Will Fly!

Watch Me Throw the Ball!

We Are in a Book!

Mo Willems is the renowned author of many award-winning books, including the Caldecott Honor winners *Don't Let the Pigeon Drive the Bus!*, *Knuffle Bunny* and *Knuffle Bunny Too*. His other groundbreaking picture books include *Knuffle Bunny Free*, *Leonardo the Terrible Monster* and *Naked Mole Rat Gets Dressed*. Before making picture books, Mo was a writer and animator on *Sesame Street*, where he won six Emmys. Mo lives with his family in Massachusetts, USA.

Visit him online at **mowillems.com** and **pigeonpresents.com**